# DEATH STAR BATTLE

WRITTEN BY TREY KING

ART BY PILOT STUDIO

DISNEY

LUCASFILM

P R E S S

Los Angeles • New York

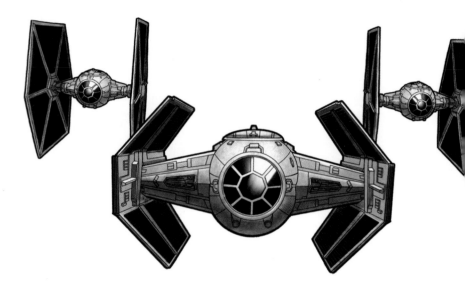

Printed in the United States of America

First Edition, February 2016

1 3 5 7 9 10 8 6 4 2

SUSTAINABLE FORESTRY INITIATIVE
Certified Sourcing
www.sfiprogram.org
SFI-01415

Library of Congress Control Number on file

G658-7729-4-15352

ISBN 978-1-4847-3148-2

Visit the official *Star Wars* website at: www.starwars.com.

Luke had always wanted to
be a good pilot.
Now the rebels needed good pilots
for a special mission.
This was Luke's chance
to prove he could help.

Luke and his friend Han had just saved
Princess Leia from Darth Vader.
Leia had secret battle plans.
The plans would help the rebels
destroy the Empire's evil weapon:
the Death Star.

Luke and his friends
flew to a moon called Yavin 4
to meet the other rebels.

The rebels looked at Leia's plans.
The plans showed that the
Death Star had one weakness.

If the rebel pilots could
fire at the weakness,
the Death Star would blow up.

But the target would be hard to hit.

Han Solo decided to leave.
The plan sounded foolish to him.
Luke tried to get him to stay,
but Han left anyway.

Luke was sad. He missed
his teacher, Obi-Wan Kenobi.
Obi-Wan would have known
what to do.

But Luke was not alone
on the mission.
His friend R2-D2
was his copilot.

Other brave pilots flew
with Luke in their X-wings.

The Death Star was near.
It was as big as a moon!

The pilots checked in
with each other.
They were ready to attack.

The Death Star's weakness
was deep inside a trench.
As the pilots neared the trench,
cannons fired at them.

Luke shot back. He destroyed
one of the cannons.
But there were still too many.

The X-wings were under attack.
TIE fighters flew down behind them.

Darth Vader led
the TIE fighters.
He wanted to protect the
Death Star at any cost.

One of the rebel pilots was
close to the target.
He fired . . .

. . . but he missed.

Leia and C-3PO were on Yavin 4.
They worried about their friends.
They also worried about the plan.

If the Death Star got too close
to Yavin 4, it would blow up
the rebel base. It was up to Luke.

Luke tried to use the X-wing's
computer to make the shot.
He was nervous.

But he heard a voice in his head.
*Use the Force, Luke.*
It was Obi-Wan.

Darth Vader was right behind Luke.
He was about to fire at Luke's ship.
Would Luke make it?

Han Solo's ship flew up behind
the TIE fighters and fired!
Han had changed his mind.
He was helping the rebels.

Han saved his friend Luke.

Vader's ship was damaged,
and it spun out into space.

Han told Luke that he was safe.
Luke could take the shot.
Luke closed his eyes
and used the Force.
Luke fired.
He hit the target.

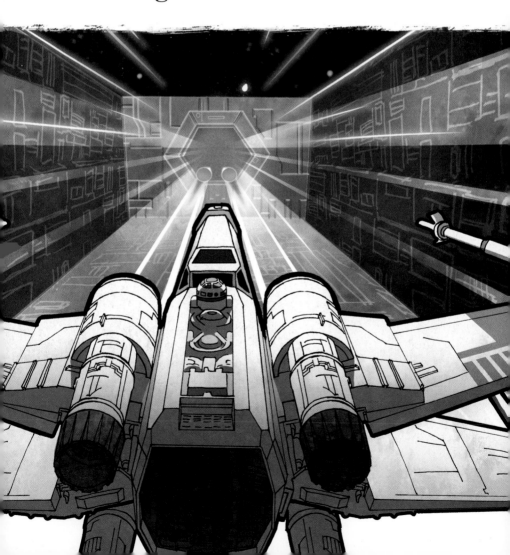

The Death Star exploded!

Luke heard the voice in his head again. *Remember,* Obi-Wan said, *the Force will be with you always.*

Back on Yavin 4, Han, Luke, and Leia
hugged each other.
They had done it.
They had beaten the Empire.

Luke had proven
he was a good pilot.
And with help from his friends,
Luke had saved the galaxy!